THE PHENOMENAL LEADER IN ME

LUCIE S. MATSOUAKA

The Phenomenal Leader In Me. Copyright © 2023 Lucie S. Matsouaka

All Rights Reserved. Printed in the United States of America.

No part of this book may be used or reproduced in any manner whatsoever without written permission except in the case of brief quotations embodied in critical articles and reviews.

Editing and Cover Design by Ruth E. Griffin/Studio Griffin, LLC.

Illustrations by Evgeniia Lanskikh

First Edition

ISBN-13: 978-1-0881-5150-1

Library of Congress Control Number: 2023940662

1 2 3 4 5 6 7 8 9 10

*To Every Child Who
Aspires To Change The World*

CONTENTS

Introduction	1
Attitude	3
Authenticity	6
Bravery	9
Choices	12
Compassion	15
Compliment	18
Creativity	21
Determination	25
Empathy	29
Faith	32
Hard Work	35
Honesty	38
Hope	42
Humility	45
Impact	48
Integrity	51
Kindness	54
Optimism	58
Patience	62
Perseverance	65

Politeness	68
Reading	72
Respect	76
Self-Care	80
Self-Confidence	83
Self-Discipline	87
Self-Esteem	91
Service	94
Conclusion	99
About The Author	101

The Phenomenal Leader In Me

INTRODUCTION

Hello Dear!

I'm your friend, Lucie.

Have you ever wondered what makes a leader great or phenomenal? What qualities do great leaders possess that set them apart from others?

I had so many hopes, dreams, and aspirations when I was your age. I dreamt of one day being in a position to make some changes in society. Just like you, I was eager to become an adult, so I could have the power to do what I wanted. What I didn't know is that phenomenal leaders have something that others don't: they have exceptional qualities. Some of these qualities are taught to us by our parents, teachers, spiritual leaders and other adults who love and take care of us. Others are learned from great books, documentaries, podcasts, or even everyday life. The most important thing that I overlooked is that I didn't have to wait until I was an adult to become a leader. I could have started a long time ago, with what I knew and what I had, to create a positive impact in the lives of those who surrounded me every single day. Would you like to know how you can do that?

Well, you're in for a treat! This book is all about the amazing qualities of the exceptional leader you will become. Let's embark on a journey to explore the characteristics that make a leader stand out. You will learn about courage, integrity, hard work, and many other traits that awesome leaders possess. I suggest you read one story every night before going to bed and then discuss what you've learned with someone (for instance, a parent or an older sibling).

By the end of this book, you'll have a better understanding of what it takes to be a leader. Are you ready to become the phenomenal leader you were born to be?

Welcome to the world of leadership!

The Phenomenal Leader In Me

ATTITUDE

Once upon a time, there was a little girl named Anna. She was always grumpy and complained about everything. She would complain about the weather, the food, and even her toys. Her friends and family tried to cheer her up, but nothing worked.

Anna's mother took her to the park for a picnic one day. They spread out a blanket, sat together, and began to eat their sandwiches. Suddenly, it started to rain, and Anna's mother suggested they pack up and go home. But Anna was unhappy and started complaining about the rain ruining their picnic.

As they walked home, they saw a group of kids playing in the rain, laughing, and having a great time. Anna's mother suggested they join in and play in the rain too. At first, Anna was hesitant, but she decided to give it a try.

To her surprise, she found that playing in the rain was fun! She laughed and smiled and felt a sense of joy she had never felt before. She realized that having a good attitude made all the difference. She no longer complained about the weather and instead looked for ways to have fun, no matter what.

Anna's mother was so proud of her that she made new friends. Anna learned the importance of having a good attitude, and how it could change her whole day.

THE END

The Phenomenal Leader In Me

Example in Real Life

Nelson Mandela was an important leader who lived in a country called South Africa. One of the things that made him a great leader was his positive attitude. Even though he spent twenty-seven years in prison, he never gave up hope. He believed in forgiveness and working together to make things better.

Mandela's positive attitude helped him to be a good leader in many ways. People trusted him and wanted to follow him.

Overall, Mandela's positive attitude was really important for his leadership. It helped him build relationships with people, keep their support, and make positive changes in South Africa. His attitude showed that even in difficult situations, having a good outlook and being kind and understanding can help make a difference.

Lucie S. Matsouaka

AUTHENTICITY

The Phenomenal Leader In Me

Once upon a time, there was a little bird named Tweet. Tweet loved to sing and chirp, but he was never quite satisfied with his voice. He wanted to sound just like the other birds in the forest, so he copied their songs and tried to sing just like them.

One day, Tweet was singing with all the other birds when a beautiful song caught his ear. It was the most beautiful song he had ever heard, and it was sung by a small bird named Birdie. Birdie had a sweet and melodic voice, and Tweet was envious. He decided to try and sing just like Birdie, so he started copying her every note. But no matter how hard he tried, he just couldn't get it right. The other birds started to notice, and they didn't like it. They told Tweet that he was being a copycat and that he should just sing his own song.

Tweet was confused. He didn't understand why it was wrong to sing like someone else. But then he realized that the voices he admired were beautiful because they were unique, and that he should be proud of his own voice.

So, the next day, Tweet sang his own song, and it was beautiful. The other birds loved it, telling him how amazing he was. Tweet was so happy and felt proud of himself. He learned that being authentic was the most important thing and that he should never try to be someone he wasn't.

From then on, Tweet sang his own songs with pride. He was finally happy and satisfied with who he was.

THE END

Question

How can you practice being more authentic in your everyday life?

_____

_____

_____

_____

_____

_____

_____

_____

_____

_____

The Phenomenal Leader In Me

BRAVERY

Once upon a time, a little girl named Sarah lived in a small village. Sarah was a kind and gentle soul, but she was also very shy and afraid of many things. One day while walking through the forest, Sarah stumbled upon a wounded dog. The dog was too injured to walk and in desperate need of help.

Sarah was scared and didn't know what to do. She was afraid of getting too close to the dog and getting hurt herself. But then she remembered an old saying that her mother used to tell her: "Bravery is not the absence of fear, but the triumph over it." Sarah realized that it would be brave of her to help the dog, despite how scared she was.

With a deep breath, Sarah approached the dog slowly. She picked it up gently and held it close to her chest. She then carried the dog back to her village, where she took care of it and helped it get better. Over time, the dog got stronger and was able to walk again.

Sarah was proud of herself for being brave and helping the dog. She learned that bravery is not just about facing physical danger, but also about facing your fears and doing the right thing, even if it's difficult.

From that day on, Sarah was not afraid to face her fears and help others. The dog she saved even became her lifelong friend and would often visit her.

THE END

The Phenomenal Leader In Me

Example in Real Life

Martin Luther King Jr. was an African American civil rights leader who fought for equal rights for Black people in America during the 1950s and 1960s. He was very brave because he stood up against unfair laws and treatment of Black people, even when it was dangerous for him to do so.

King led peaceful protests and demonstrations to raise awareness about the discrimination and segregation that Black people faced. He gave powerful speeches, like his famous "I Have a Dream" speech, that inspired many people to join the fight for civil rights.

King faced a lot of opposition and was often met with violence from those who disagreed with him. He was arrested many times, and his house was even bombed. Despite these dangers, he continued to fight for what he believed was right and never gave up.

In the end, King's bravery and leadership helped bring about important changes to America's laws and society. He is remembered today as a hero who fought for justice and equality for all people.

Lucie S. Matsouaka

CHOICES

The Phenomenal Leader In Me

Once upon a time, there was a little girl named Lisa. Lisa loved nothing more than spending time with her friends, but one day, her friends invited her to do something that made her feel uncomfortable.

Lisa's friends wanted to sneak into the neighborhood pool after hours and swim. Lisa knew that this was wrong and could get them all in trouble, but she didn't want to disappoint her friends, so she went along with it.

As they were swimming and having fun, a security guard caught them and called their parents. Lisa felt ashamed and guilty. Her parents were disappointed in her. She knew she had made a bad choice by going along with her friends.

The next day at school, Lisa's friends were bragging about what had happened. She asked, "Don't you feel guilty? Don't you feel ashamed?" Her friends responded, "No, it wasn't that serious!" Lisa knew she couldn't go along with them again, so she made the difficult decision to tell them that she couldn't be a part of their plans anymore. They were upset with her, but Lisa knew it was the right thing to do.

When Lisa went home, she told her parents, and they were very proud of her for making the right choice. She felt relieved that she no longer had to hide anything from them or feel guilty. She found new friends who shared her values and didn't pressure her to do things she knew were wrong.

As she grew older, Lisa continued to make choices that were true to her values, even when it was difficult. She learned that making the right choice not only felt good but also helped her build strong relationships with people who respected her for who she was.

THE END

Example in Real Life

Martin Luther King Jr. had to make many tough choices in his life as a leader in the Civil Rights Movement. One of the hardest choices was deciding to speak up for the rights of African Americans, even though it was dangerous. He also had to choose how to protest without violence, even when others used violent tactics.

Sometimes King didn't agree with other leaders' methods, but he still respected them. King also had to balance his duties as a husband and father with his responsibilities as a public figure.

Despite all these tough choices, King never stopped fighting for equality. He believed it was important to use his voice and influence to make a better world, even when it was difficult and sometimes scary.

The Phenomenal Leader In Me

COMPASSION

Once upon a time, there was a little boy named Toby. He was smart and strong but also very mean to others. He would always make fun of the kids who were different from him and never showed any kindness to anyone.

One day, while he was walking home from school, he saw a little kitten who was lost and sad. He was about to walk away when he heard the kitten's meows. He stopped and thought about how the kitten must be feeling, and he realized that it must be scared and lonely.

Toby felt a warm feeling in his heart, and he decided to help the kitten. He lifted the kitten in his arms and took it home. He gave it some food and water and played with it. Toby asked his parents to help him find the kitten's owners. They looked everywhere, posted signs in the neighborhood, and asked all their neighbors if they recognized the kitten.

A few days later, they came across a little girl named Cheng. Cheng was sobbing. She was sitting on a small rock with a sign reading, "If you find a kitten, please call the number below…" Toby ran to her and said, "I think I have your kitten. Follow me, and I'll show you." They went to Toby's house and the little girl jumped with excitement once she saw the kitten, ecstatic after having finally found it after many days of searching. Toby smiled and said, "You can take it home. I took good care of it." They both became good friends, with Cheng promising to come to visit him with the kitten.

From that day on, Toby learned the importance of having compassion for others. He found that he was much happier when he helped others. He realized that helping others can bring joy and happiness to both the giver and the receiver.

THE END

Example in Real Life

Mother Teresa was a remarkable leader who showed compassion to all those around her. She dedicated her life to helping the poor, sick, and marginalized people of the world. She is a great example of how we can all lead with compassion in our own lives.

Mother Teresa's compassion was evident in everything she did. She lived a simple life and put the needs of others before her own. She would often go out of her way to help people, even if it meant sacrificing her own comfort. She believed that every person was valuable and deserved to be treated with dignity and respect.

One of Mother Teresa's most famous quotes is, "Not all of us can do great things. But we can do small things with great love." This quote sums up her approach to life and leadership. She believed that even the smallest act of kindness could make a big difference in someone's life.

Lucie S. Matsouaka

COMPLIMENT

The Phenomenal Leader In Me

Once upon a time, in a magical forest, there lived a group of animals. One day, while they were playing, a new animal joined their group. He introduced himself. "Hi! I'm Peter, the rabbit." Peter was very kind and always had something nice to say about the other animals.

Days passed and Peter decided to live there with the other animals. He often complimented them on their unique features and talents. He told the birds how beautiful their songs were and the squirrels how fast and nimble they were. His compliments were always sincere; and left the other animals feeling appreciated and valued.

One day, the animals noticed that Peter was feeling sad and no longer wanted to play. They gathered around him and asked what was wrong. Peter responded, "I don't feel like I belong in the group." The other animals were surprised because they thought Peter was one of the kindest animals they had ever met. One of them said, "Of course you belong here! We're all much better since you came." Peter said, "I had no idea. I thought I was not important to you."

The animals realized that they were taking Peter for granted. They were too busy having fun and forgot to appreciate Peter's qualities. They apologized and started to give him heartfelt compliments. They told him how his kindness and compassion made the forest a better place.

Peter felt happy and accepted once again. From that day on, the animals in the magical forest made it a point to give genuine compliments to each other. They realized that a simple compliment could brighten someone's day and make them feel valued and appreciated.

THE END

Lucie S. Matsouaka

Question

When was a time you gave compliments to someone?

The Phenomenal Leader In Me

CREATIVITY

Once upon a time, in a magical place called the Imagination Kingdom, there lived a group of happy creatures known as the "Creatives." These Creatives had the power to bring their wildest dreams to life, simply by using their imagination and creativity.

One day, the Creatives were getting ready for their annual Creativity Festival, a grand celebration where they would showcase their most amazing creations. However, as the day approached, they realized that something was wrong—their creativity seemed to have vanished!

Panic spread across the Imagination Kingdom, as the Creatives desperately searched for a way to bring back their creativity. They tried all their usual methods, but nothing seemed to work. It looked like the Creativity Festival would have to be canceled, and the Creatives were really sad.

Just then, a little girl named Mia stumbled upon the Creatives' plight. Mia was a curious and imaginative child, and she knew just what to do. She gathered all the Creatives together and suggested that they try something new—they should take a walk through the forest, and let their imaginations run wild.

At first, the Creatives were unsure. They had never tried anything like this before, and they were scared it might not work. But Mia was convincing, and soon they were all wandering through the forest, imagining all sorts of wonderful things.

Suddenly, the Creatives felt something magical happening - their creativity was returning! They started to see shapes and colors that they had never seen before, and they felt more inspired than ever. When they got back to the Imagination

Kingdom, they worked really hard to create the most amazing creations they had ever made.

The Creativity Festival was a huge success, and everyone in the Imagination Kingdom was amazed by the incredible things the Creatives had done. Mia was hailed as a hero, and the Creatives knew that they had learned an important lesson. They realized that creativity was not something that could be forced or controlled—it needed to be nurtured and allowed to grow freely.

From that day on, the Creatives made sure to take regular walks through the forest, and they always made time to let their imaginations run wild. And whenever they felt their creativity slipping away, they knew just what to do—take a walk, let their imaginations soar, and watch the magic happen.

THE END

Example in Real Life

Highness Sheikh Mohammed bin Rashid Al Maktoum, the Vice President, and Prime Minister of the United Arab Emirates (UAE), is widely known for his innovative and creative leadership style. He has used his creativity to make his country successful and famous around the world.

One of the things that Sheikh Mohammed did was to come up with big ideas to make Dubai a great place to visit and do business. For example, he built the world's tallest building, called the Burj Khalifa, an artificial island that looks like a palm tree, and one of the largest shopping centers in the world, called the Dubai Mall. These projects have helped Dubai to become a popular tourist destination and attract businesses from all over the world.

Sheikh Mohammed also started a school called the Mohammed bin Rashid School of Government, which teaches people how to be leaders in the government. This school has special programs that teach students things like how to be a good leader, how to plan for the future, and how to make good policies.

The Phenomenal Leader In Me

DETERMINATION

Once upon a time, there was a little girl named Chloe. She lived in a small town with her parents and siblings. Chloe was different from other kids in her town as she had a big dream. She wanted to be a famous singer and travel the world to spread happiness and joy through her music.

But the problem was that Chloe was not born with a great voice. She had a thin and weak voice which nobody liked, causing people to laugh at her whenever she tried to sing. However, Chloe was not discouraged by their laughter. She was determined to follow her dream of becoming a famous singer.

Every day, she would practice singing for hours. She would sing in front of a mirror, imagining herself performing in front of a huge audience. She would try different techniques to make her voice stronger and more melodious.

Years passed and Chloe's hard work and determination paid off. Her voice became stronger, and she started to win singing competitions at her school. All the students were amazed at how she had transformed from a shy, weak-voiced girl to a confident, strong-voiced singer.

One day, Chloe received an invitation to perform in the capital city. She was nervous, but she was also excited about the opportunity to showcase her talent. When the day of the performance arrived, Chloe stepped on the stage with determination. She closed her eyes and began to sing. The audience was stunned. Chloe's voice was so beautiful; they couldn't believe the sheer talent of the little girl they once laughed at.

Chloe's performance was a huge success; she was soon invited to perform in other cities and states. She traveled, spreading joy through her music. She became a famous singer, just like she had dreamed of.

Chloe's determination and hard work inspired many people. They learned that with determination, anything is possible.

THE END

Question

How can you be more determined in your everyday life?

_____

_____

_____

_____

_____

_____

_____

_____

_____

_____

_____

The Phenomenal Leader In Me

EMPATHY

Once upon a time, in a magical land, there was a little boy named Ahmad. He had many friends, but there was one thing that he lacked—empathy. He didn't understand what others felt and didn't care about their feelings. He only thought of himself.

One day, Ahmad stumbled upon a mouse who was crying on the side of the road. He asked, "Why are you crying?" The mouse replied, "I have lost my family and I have nowhere to go." Ahmad thought about it for a moment and said, "Oh, that's too bad. I have to go now." And he walked away without a second thought.

As he walked, he came across another sad creature, this time a raccoon. He asked, "What's the matter?" The raccoon replied, "I have lost my best friend and I feel very lonely." Ahmad again thought about it for a moment and said, "That's too bad. I have to go now." And he walked away without a second thought.

Ahmad continued on his way, and as he walked, he thought to himself, "Why is everyone sad? Is there anything I could have done to make them feel better? Maybe I should have not ignored them." He felt so ashamed.

He decided to go back and apologize to each of the creatures he had met. He listened to their stories and tried to understand what they were feeling. He hugged them and comforted them, and soon everyone's sadness had turned into happiness.

Ahmad learned a valuable lesson that day: having empathy means putting yourself in someone else's shoes and caring about their feelings. When we have empathy, we can make others happy and spread kindness around us.

THE END

Example in Real Life

Kwame Nkrumah was a leader who wanted everyone to understand and care about each other. He believed that if we can feel empathy, we can create a society where everyone is treated fairly and equally. He worked to create a sense of togetherness among people from different backgrounds and encouraged Ghana to help other African countries.

Nkrumah believed that leaders should be able to understand and connect with the experiences and needs of their people. This way, leaders can build trust and support among the people they lead. He thought that empathy is not just something individuals have, but it's also an essential part of a healthy and fair society.

Lucie S. Matsouaka

FAITH

The Phenomenal Leader In Me

Once upon a time, there was a little boy named Jeff. Jeff loved learning and discovering new things. He worked very hard in school, but sometimes things didn't go as planned.

One day, Jeff was working on a school project on his computer. He had spent a lot of time researching and writing. Suddenly, his computer crashed! He was so sad and upset because he had lost everything he had worked on.

But Jeff's parents reminded him that even when things go wrong, we should keep trying and not give up. They told him to have faith in himself and God; and keep working hard.

So, Jeff decided to start over and work even harder than before. He spent lots of time researching and writing again, and he finally finished his project. He was very proud of himself!

Jeff learned that even when things go wrong, we should never give up. If we work hard and keep trying, we can achieve anything we want. He knew that he could always keep the faith and keep going, no matter what challenges he faced.

From that day on, Jeff never gave up on his dreams, and he always remembered the importance of keeping the faith. And he knew that you can do it too if you believe in yourself and never give up!

THE END

Example in Real Life

Denzel Washington is a famous actor who believes that faith is really important. He thinks that having faith in God and in yourself can help you do great things and get through tough times. He learned about faith from his mom, who taught him to believe in himself and in God. He also believes that praying can help you feel less scared and more confident.

Denzel was in a movie called, "The Book of Eli", which is about faith and doing the right thing. He has also helped out with a group called the Boys & Girls Clubs of America, which is based on faith and helping kids.

The Phenomenal Leader In Me

HARD WORK

Once upon a time, there was a little ant named Annie. Annie lived in a big ant colony and all the ants worked very hard every day. They would go out early in the morning and collect food for the colony.

One day, Annie was feeling lazy and didn't want to work. She thought, "Why should I work so hard? Everyone else is doing it, so I don't have to." So, she sat and watched as all the other ants worked.

But soon, she noticed that the colony was not getting enough food. Many ants were hungry and tired. Annie felt guilty for not doing her part. She decided to get up and help.

Soon, she collected more and more food. Her contribution was felt by the other ants. They felt relieved as with Annie's help, the colony was able to work a little faster and they were able to accumulate more food for later.

Annie was proud of her hard work and decided to always work when it was time to work and rest when it was time to rest. The other ants were proud of her too and admired her for her determination and dedication. She understood that it is important to do your part to help others.

THE END

The Phenomenal Leader In Me

Example in Real Life

Lee Kuan Yew was a leader in Singapore who believed in the importance of working hard. He helped Singapore become a successful and prosperous country by encouraging people to work hard and learn new skills. Lee Kuan Yew said that working hard, saving money, and taking care of others were important values that helped Singapore grow. He also thought that leaders should work hard and set a good example for others.

Under Lee Kuan Yew's leadership, Singapore made changes to help people go to school, start their own businesses, and come up with new ideas. This made people in Singapore want to work hard and do their best. Now, Singapore is one of the most successful and competitive countries in the world, and it's because of the hard work and dedication of its people, inspired by Lee Kuan Yew.

Lucie S. Matsouaka

HONESTY

The Phenomenal Leader In Me

Once upon a time, in a rural village, there lived a boy named Arnold. Arnold was always known for his mischievous nature and his love for telling lies. His friends and family members were tired of his lies and were always scolding him for his behavior.

One day, Arnold and his friends decided to go on a treasure hunt. They searched everywhere, and finally, Arnold found a chest full of gold coins. He was very excited and decided to keep the treasure all to himself. So, he lied to his friends and told them that the chest was empty.

The next day, Arnold went to the market to buy himself some sweets with the money he had stolen. But, as he was about to buy the sweets, he noticed that he had lost the money. He was very upset and worried, so he decided to go to the village chief for help. He forgot that no one knew that he had the coins.

The village chief listened carefully to Arnold's story and asked, "Where did you get those coins from?"

"My uncle is very rich. He gave them to me," Arnold said.

The village chief looked him in the eyes and said, "Be honest, young man."

Arnold was ashamed. He looked down and finally confessed that he had lied to his friends about the treasure and that he had stolen the money. The village chief was very disappointed in Arnold, but said, "You're forgiven this time, but don't do that again."

Arnold promised to always tell the truth. The chief ordered some people to help him look for the money. Arnold had misplaced it and didn't remember where he put it. They found the stolen money and he ran to talk to his friends and apologize for his behavior. His friends forgave him as well and they became close friends again.

Arnold learned a valuable lesson that day. He realized that being honest and truthful was the key to having a good relationship with others. He was happy and proud of himself for making the right choice.

THE END

Example in Real Life

Thomas Sankara was a leader who ruled Burkina Faso, a country in Africa, from 1983 to 1987. He was known for being an honest leader who worked hard to improve the lives of his people. Sankara fought against corruption, which is when people in power use their position to do dishonest things. He did things like selling expensive cars that the government didn't really need and using the money for more important things that could help people, like building schools and clinics in rural areas.

Sankara also cared a lot about the environment and the health of the people in Burkina Faso. He started a campaign to plant trees to help stop the spread of deserts and he made sure everyone had access to vaccinations to stay healthy.

Sankara was also a big supporter of other African countries and their struggles for freedom. He didn't like foreign countries giving aid or money to African countries because he thought it made them dependent on others. Instead, he wanted African countries to be independent and strong on their own.

Sadly, Sankara was assassinated in 1987, but he is remembered as a hero to the people of Burkina Faso and Africa because of his honesty, hard work, and commitment to making life better for his people.

Lucie S. Matsouaka

HOPE

The Phenomenal Leader In Me

Once upon a time, a little girl named Elikya loved to dream big. She had many hopes and aspirations, but she often felt discouraged when things didn't go as planned.

One day, Elikya was feeling particularly down after she had failed a test at school. She sat on a bench in the playground and started to cry. Suddenly, a teacher walked up to her and asked what was wrong. Elikya told her about the test and how she felt like giving up on her dreams.

The teacher smiled and said, "Elikya, my dear, don't be discouraged. The journey to your dreams may not be easy, but it will be worth it in the end. Always remember to keep your hope and faith strong. Believe in yourself and you will see that anything is possible."

Elikya felt a little better after hearing the teacher's words. She dried her tears and stood up. The teacher said, "Before you go, promise me to never give up on your dreams, no matter what obstacles you face. Elikya smiled and said, "I promise!" She went back to studying with a new determination.

Years went by and Elikya worked hard and never lost hope. She remembered to be hopeful and never give up on her dreams. She believed that with hard work and determination, anything was possible.

Elikya eventually graduated from college with honors and got her dream job as a scientist. She was grateful for the teacher's words of encouragement.

THE END

Example in Real Life

Barack Obama, a former US president, thinks that hope is really important. He believes that hope is a strong feeling that can help people make good things happen. He often talks about how it's important to have hope, especially when things are hard. He thinks that hope isn't just about feeling good, but about helping people create a better future.

When Obama ran for president in 2008, he used the slogan "Yes We Can" to show that everyone working together can make big changes. During his time as president, he talked a lot about how it's important to stay hopeful, even when things are tough.

Basically, Obama believes that hope is powerful and can help people do amazing things, even when they face challenges.

The Phenomenal Leader In Me

HUMILITY

Once upon a time, a young boy named Johan lived in the city. Johan was very talented and smart. He could do anything he wanted and always came first in his class. But as he got older, he started to become arrogant and believed that he was better than everyone else.

One day, Johan was walking home from school when he saw a group of students talking about the last test and how they wished they understood mathematics better. Johan overheard their conversation and laughed at them. He said, "You're clearly not studying hard enough. You ought to be more like me. I study, but I'm also smart." They looked at him with disgust and responded, "You shouldn't make fun of others just because you know something they don't." Johan pretended not to hear anything and walked away smirking.

The next day, Johan went to the fair and saw a man performing amazing tricks. Johan decided to show off his skills by doing a trick that was much harder. But as soon as Johan started, he stumbled and fell. The crowd laughed and Johan felt embarrassed.

The man came over to him and said, "Young man, being humble is more important than being talented. When you are humble, people respect you and want to be around you. But if you remain arrogant, people will avoid you and you will be lonely."

Johan realized the error of his ways and felt sorry for the way he had been treating people. He decided to change for the better. The following day in school, he started to change his attitude. It didn't take long before Johan started to make new friends.

THE END

Example in Real Life

Patrice Lumumba was a really important leader in the Democratic Republic of the Congo. He was the first person to be elected as their leader by the people, which is a big deal! What made Lumumba special was that he was really humble and cared about his country and the people who lived there.

When Lumumba became the leader, he didn't want a big fancy ceremony like most leaders usually have. He wanted a simple ceremony that showed he cared more about the people than about showing off.

Lumumba knew that no one person could solve all of the problems in the Congo, so he worked with other people to make decisions. He wanted everyone to help and be a part of making the Congo better.

In summary, Patrice Lumumba was a really great leader who was humble, cared about his country and people, and wanted everyone to work together to make things better.

Lucie S. Matsouaka

IMPACT

The Phenomenal Leader In Me

Once upon a time, there was a young girl named Victoria. She lived in a small town surrounded by lush green forests and rolling hills. Despite the beauty of her surroundings, Victoria felt that something was missing in her life. She wanted to make a difference and leave a lasting impact on her community.

One day, while exploring the nearby forest, Victoria stumbled upon a group of animals struggling to find food and water. The stream that once flowed freely was now nearly dry, and the trees that provided shade and nourishment were being cut down. Victoria realized that these changes were caused by humans and that something had to be done to help the animals and the environment.

Victoria went back to her town and gathered her friends to discuss what they could do. They decided to plant trees and clean up the stream to bring life back to the forest. They also spread the word about the importance of conservation and the need to protect the environment.

The town came together and worked hard to transform the forest. After a while, the animals began to return, and the streams flowed once again. They were all proud of their work and felt a sense of fulfillment knowing they made a positive impact.

Years passed, and the fruits of Victoria and her friends' labor could be seen all around. The forests were lush and full of life, the streams flowed freely, and the animals thrived. They had made a positive impact in their community.

Victoria and her friends learned that no matter how small or young you are, you have the power to make a lasting impact on the world. Victoria encouraged others to find ways to make a difference and leave their mark on the world.

THE END

Example in Real Life

Dr. Myles Munroe was a very special person who helped lots of people learn how to be better leaders and achieve their dreams. He was born in a country called the Bahamas in 1954 and sadly passed away in 2014. He taught people that anyone can be a great leader, no matter where they come from or what they do. He also believed that every person has a special purpose in life and that by finding and following that purpose, they can be happy and successful. He wrote lots of books about how to be a better leader and how to live a happy life. He was very popular, and his books have been read by many people all around the world.

Dr. Munroe made a big difference in people's lives by inspiring them to believe in themselves and work hard to achieve their dreams. Even though he is no longer with us, his ideas and teachings continue to help people become better leaders and find success in their lives.

The Phenomenal Leader In Me

INTEGRITY

Once upon a time, in a far-off kingdom, there was a king named Daniel who ruled with fairness and justice. He was loved and respected by all his subjects. One day, the kingdom was facing a major crisis. The crops were failing, and the people were suffering. The king had to make a tough decision to help his people.

Daniel knew that there was a large amount of gold stored in the royal treasury, and he could use it to buy food for the people. However, he also knew that using the royal treasury for personal gain was against the rules of the kingdom. He had to choose between helping his people and breaking the rules.

Daniel gathered all his advisors to discuss the situation. He told them about his dilemma and asked for their opinions. They all agreed that using the gold from the treasury was the only way to save the kingdom. However, Daniel decided against it. He knew that breaking the rules would set a bad example for the people and future kings. He didn't want to sacrifice his integrity for the sake of a temporary solution.

After thinking about it for a few days, the king came up with a new plan. He called upon the wealthy merchants of the kingdom and asked for their help. He told them about the crisis and asked for a loan to buy food for the people. The merchants were impressed by Daniel's honesty and integrity and agreed to help.

In no time, the food was distributed to the people, and the crisis was averted. Daniel's subjects were even more impressed by his leadership and integrity. They admired him for making the right decision in a tough time.

From that day on, Daniel's legacy was remembered as the king who ruled with fairness, justice, and integrity.

THE END

The Phenomenal Leader In Me

Example in Real Life

Nelson Mandela was a South African anti-apartheid revolutionary and political leader who led with integrity. He spent twenty-seven years in prison for his activism but never compromised on his principles of justice, equality, and reconciliation. He believed in being honest and telling the truth, even when it was hard. He was also very humble, and never thought he was better than anyone else. He was always consistent in what he believed and what he did, even when things were difficult.

Mandela was also really good at forgiving people who had hurt him or his friends. He knew that forgiveness was important for people to get along.

All of these things made people trust and respect Mandela. He helped make the world a better place.

Lucie S. Matsouaka

KINDNESS

The Phenomenal Leader In Me

Once upon a time, in a small school called Kindness Elementary School, there were many students. They loved to learn and play. However, there was a problem in the school, and that was that some students were not kind to others. The principal had named the school "Kindness" because he wanted all his students to embody the word that was dear to his heart.

One day, a new student named Afia joined the class. She was shy and didn't know anyone in the class. When she walked into the classroom, some students whispered to each other and giggled at her. Afia felt embarrassed and didn't know how to react.

The next day, during recess, Afia was sitting alone, watching other students playing. A boy named Kofi came to her and asked her if she wanted to play with him and his friends. Afia was hesitant at first, but Kofi was so kind that she agreed to play with them. They had a great time, and Afia was happy to have made new friends.

As the days passed, Kofi and his friends continued to include Afia in their activities. They even helped her with her homework and showed her around the school. Afia was no longer alone and had a wonderful time in school.

One day, the principal announced that there would be a competition to see which class had the kindest students. Kofi and his friends came up with a plan. They decided to include everyone in their activities and make sure no one was left out. They also helped other students with their work and showed kindness in every possible way.

Finally, the day of the competition arrived, and the principal announced that Kofi's class had won. Everyone cheered, and the principal congratulated them for their kindness. He gave them a bag of candy to share among themselves.

The next day, the school principal announced that the school would be holding a Kindness Day. Everyone in the school was to show an act of kindness to someone else. Kofi and his friends were thrilled and came up with many ideas to spread kindness around the school.

That day, everyone in the school showed kindness to each other. They helped each other with their work, shared their lunch, and played together. It was a beautiful day, and everyone felt happy and loved.

From that day on, everyone in the school made a promise to be kind to each other. They realized that kindness makes everyone happy and that being kind is the right thing to do. Afia was no longer the new kid in school but a happy and confident student who had so many friends.

The moral of the story is that being kind is essential in school as well as everywhere else. Kindness makes people feel happy and loved. So, always be kind to others, and you will see how wonderful the world can be!

THE END

The Phenomenal Leader In Me

Example in Real Life

Tyler Perry is a famous actor, writer, and director, who is also known for being really kind, which is one of the things that makes him a great leader.

He's always helping out people who need it, like giving money to groups that help those affected by natural disasters or domestic violence. He also supports new actors and writers by giving them opportunities to be in his productions and helping them improve their skills.

Tyler Perry also thinks it's important to have people from all backgrounds in movies and television shows, and he makes sure to include lots of different kinds of people in his work.

Overall, Tyler Perry's kindness and caring nature are what make him an awesome leader and a good role model.

Lucie S. Matsouaka

OPTIMISM

The Phenomenal Leader In Me

Once upon a time, there was a little rabbit named Rosie. She lived in a beautiful meadow, filled with colorful flowers and tall green grass. Rosie loved to hop around and play with her friends, but sometimes she felt sad and worried about the future.

One day, Rosie was feeling particularly down. She had heard that a big storm was coming, and she was scared that it would ruin her home and destroy all the flowers in the meadow. She sat by herself under a tree, feeling gloomy and hopeless.

As she sat there, she saw an owl flying towards her. The owl perched on a branch above her and asked, "Why do you look so sad, little Rosie?"

Rosie told the owl about her fears and worries. The owl listened carefully and then said, "I understand that you're afraid of what might happen, but it's important to remember that the storm might not be as bad as you think. And even if it is, you can still find joy and happiness in other things in the world."

Rosie looked up at the owl, unsure of what to think. But the owl continued, "Being optimistic means believing that good things can happen, even when things seem bleak. It means looking for the bright side of every situation and having hope for the future."

Rosie thought about what the owl had said, and she realized that she had been focusing too much on the negative. She decided to try and be more optimistic, even in the face of uncertainty.

The next day, the storm arrived. At first, Rosie was scared, but then she remembered the owl's words. She looked around her and saw that the storm was actually quite beautiful. The raindrops sparkled like diamonds, and the lightning lit up the sky in a dazzling display. She realized that even though the storm was scary, it was also magnificent in its own way.

After the storm passed, Rosie went outside and saw that the meadow was still there, just as beautiful as ever. Some flowers had been knocked down, but many more were still standing tall. Rosie realized that even though bad things happen, the world is still full of wonder and beauty.

From then on, Rosie tried to be more optimistic, even when things seemed tough. She learned that having hope and looking for the bright side of things could make all the difference. And even when things were hard, she knew that she could always find something to be grateful for.

THE END

The Phenomenal Leader In Me

Question

How can you practice being optimistic in your everyday life?

_____

_____

_____

_____

_____

_____

_____

_____

_____

_____

_____

Lucie S. Matsouaka

PATIENCE

The Phenomenal Leader In Me

Once upon a time, there was a little girl named Corazón. Corazón had a beautiful smile and a cheerful personality. However, she was impatient.

Every time she wanted something, she wanted it right away. If she had to wait, she would get frustrated and upset. Her friends and family would try to calm her down and explain that good things come to those who wait, but Corazón just didn't want to hear it.

One day after school, Corazón went to an ice cream shop with her friends. The line was long, and Corazón was getting more and more impatient. At some point, she decided to give up, get out of the line and go home. Her friends tried to persuade her to stay in line, but Corazón didn't want to hear it.

She started to walk home. Meanwhile, the other girls stayed and finally got their ice cream. Excited, they ate it, then ran back home. On their way back, they saw Corazón. She was still walking and starting to feel a little hungry. "Did you get your ice cream?" she asked them. "Yes," they said. "It was very good and refreshing. You should have waited. See? You're still on the road and we're going back home together."

Corazón felt sad and regretted not being patient enough to wait for her turn. She was hungry and thirsty, and she didn't want to go back to the ice cream shop. One of her friends opened her backpack and said, "Surprise! We bought you a cookie and a small bottle of water. But promise us you'll change your attitude." Corazón smiled, hugged them both, and promised to do so.

Corazón had learned an important lesson: patience is a virtue that will always pay off in the end.

THE END

Example in Real Life

Sidney Poitier was an actor and filmmaker who was very patient. He was careful about which roles he took on, and he only chose roles that he thought were interesting and important. This meant that he turned down some jobs, even if they offered him a lot of money because he didn't want to play characters that were stereotypical or not very interesting.

Poitier was also one of the first Black actors to become famous in Hollywood. But he didn't do it by just taking any role that was offered to him. He wanted to break down barriers and make sure that Black actors and filmmakers had more opportunities in Hollywood. This took a lot of time and patience, but he kept working hard and advocating for change. As a result, he became a role model for other Black actors and made a big impact on Hollywood. Now, many filmmakers follow in his footsteps.

The Phenomenal Leader In Me

PERSEVERANCE

Once upon a time, in a small village, there was a little boy named Imamu. Imamu was very energetic and loved to play. But, unlike other children, Imamu had a big dream. He wanted to be the best runner in the village.

Every day, Imamu would run around the village, practicing, and steadily getting better and better. But one day, Imamu fell and hurt his ankle. He was devastated and thought he would never be able to run again. His mother took him to a doctor who examined his ankle.

"My son," said the doctor, "There are no broken bones, but you need to rest for a few days before walking again. Don't put too much pressure on your foot until you feel better."

On their way home, Imamu had a bandaged ankle. He asked, "Mother, are you sure I'll be able to run again?"

"Of course, you will! You're still growing, and the body has a special way to heal itself. You just have to keep trying." She reminded him of all the hard work he had put into his running and that he couldn't give up now. Imamu listened to his mother and started to practice again when he felt better, this time very carefully and with the bandaged ankle.

Although he was slow, Imamu kept practicing every day. He didn't give up and he persevered.

One day, the village held a big running competition. Imamu entered and felt a little nervous. Then, he remembered all the encouraging words of his mother. With determination and hard work, Imamu ran faster and harder than ever before. He won the competition and was crowned the best runner in the village! Imamu learned that success takes hard work and perseverance.

THE END

The Phenomenal Leader In Me

Example in Real Life

Darren Hardy is a well-known author and speaker who talks a lot about how to be a great leader and how to do well in life. He says that if you want to be really good at something, you need to keep trying and not give up. It's important to keep going and not quit just because you face challenges.

Darren Hardy also thinks that being a great leader doesn't just happen overnight. You have to learn and grow over time, and part of that means not giving up when things get tough. When you keep trying and don't give up, you'll become a better leader, and you'll be able to help others do the same.

Finally, Darren Hardy believes that it's really important for leaders to inspire others to keep going, too. If you show your friends that you're willing to keep trying, even when things are hard, they'll be more likely to do the same. And when everyone keeps going, they can achieve amazing things together!

Lucie S. Matsouaka

POLITENESS

The Phenomenal Leader In Me

Once upon a time, there was a little boy named Liam. Liam loved playing with his toys and going on adventures in his backyard, but he didn't always remember to be polite when he met new people.

One day, Liam's family went to a party at his neighbor's house. When they arrived, Liam saw a group of kids playing together in the backyard. He ran up to them and said, "Hey, let me play too!"

But instead of saying hello and introducing himself, Liam just barged right in and grabbed one of their toys. The other kids looked at him with surprise and didn't know what to say. Liam didn't seem to care, and he started playing with the toy without asking.

After a few minutes, one of the kids said, "Hey, can I have my toy back please?" But Liam just ignored him and kept playing. Another kid said, "You're not being very nice. You should say sorry." But Liam just shrugged and kept playing.

As the party went on, Liam found himself alone and without any friends to play with. The other kids didn't want to play with him because he had been so impolite. Liam felt sad and left out, and he didn't understand why no one wanted to be his friend.

That night, when Liam was about to go to bed, he couldn't stop thinking about what happened at the party. He shared the story with his mother. She said, "Liam, these are the consequences of not being polite. We talked about this several times. You can't just ignore people when you walk into a room. Be kind. People need to feel acknowledged." He realized that he had been rude and hurt the other kids' feelings. He felt bad and wished he could go back and make things right.

The next day, Liam decided to apologize to the kids he had met at the party. He went over to their house and said, "I'm sorry for being rude yesterday. I should have said hello and asked before playing with your toys. Can we be friends now?"

The other kids smiled and said, "Of course! We're happy you said sorry." From that day on, Liam remembered to be polite wherever he went and when he met new people. He realized that being kind and respectful was important, not just for making friends, but for making the world a better place.

So, remember, kids, always say hello, introduce yourself, and ask before taking or playing with someone else's things. Being polite will help you make friends and make others feel good too. But if you're rude and impolite, you might find yourself alone and without any friends.

THE END

The Phenomenal Leader In Me

Example in Real Life

John C. Maxwell is a well-known author, speaker, and leader who teaches about how important it is to be polite. Being polite means treating others with kindness and respect, no matter who they are or where they come from. It's not just about being nice, but about building good relationships and doing well in life. He says that being polite is like having good manners. When we talk to people, we should listen carefully and try to understand them. By doing this, we can avoid problems and become friends with people.

Being polite is also important if we want to be leaders. Leaders are people who help others and make things better. They do this by being kind to others and treating them with respect. When leaders are polite, people feel happy and work better together.

Lucie S. Matsouaka

READING

The Phenomenal Leader In Me

Once upon a time, a young girl named Angel lived in a suburban town. She loved spending time with her friends and playing outside, but she wasn't very fond of reading. She found books boring and never picked one up unless she was forced to do so.

One day, her mother took her to the local library and introduced her to the librarian, Mrs. Smith. Mrs. Smith showed Angel around the library and told her about all the wonderful books they had. Angel was still not interested in reading, but Mrs. Smith wouldn't give up.

"Angel, reading is one of the most important things you can do," Mrs. Smith said. "It opens up a whole new world, filled with adventure, magic, and amazing stories."

Angel was skeptical, but Mrs. Smith promised her that if she read one good book, she would see the magic for herself. So, Angel reluctantly picked up a book about a brave knight and his quest to save a princess from a dragon. As she began reading, she was transported to a new world filled with magic and adventure. The more she read, the more she was captivated by the story. When she finished the book, she ran back to the bookshelves to get another one.

When her mother came to pick her up, she ran to her and said, "Mom, I never knew books could be so much fun! Can we return to the library tomorrow, please? I want to read more and more and learn all sorts of new things."

From that day on, Angel was a reading enthusiast. She spent the next few weeks reading all sorts of books about talking animals, magical kingdoms, and far-away planets. Books became a gateway to a world of imagination and creativity for her. Angel learned that books were full of excitement and wonder, and she realized the importance of reading good books. She was expanding her mind, broadening her horizons, and enriching her vocabulary. Her mother was so proud of her.

THE END

The Phenomenal Leader In Me

Example in Real Life

Oprah Winfrey is a person who really loves books and wants to tell everyone how awesome they are. She even started a book club in 1996 to share good book recommendations with others. She thinks books are super cool because they can take you on adventures and teach you about different people and places. She says that reading can help you understand and care about others, even if they are very different from you.

Reading has also helped Oprah a lot in her life. She calls books her "personal mentors" because they have taught her many things and helped her find her own voice.

So, if you want to learn new things, go on adventures, and have fun. Oprah thinks you should read more books!

Lucie S. Matsouaka

RESPECT

The Phenomenal Leader In Me

Once upon a time, there was a little boy named Caleb. He was very playful and loved to run around and have fun with his friends. But he had a habit of being rude and unkind to others.

One day at school, Caleb was playing with his friends when he saw a new girl. He didn't like the way the new girl looked and started making fun of her. His friends followed his lead and soon the new girl was surrounded by a group of mean kids. They were making fun of her and bullying her. Feeling sad, the new girl ran away. They started laughing even louder.

The next day, Caleb saw her and called his friends. They started to mock her again, and again, and again. Caleb was enjoying being mean and disrespectful to the new girl at school.

One day, at recess, he was about to approach her when she screamed, "Stay away from me! You're very annoying." Luckily that day, a teacher saw everything through the windows. Caleb was called into the office to explain himself. He felt a twinge of guilt and asked for forgiveness. The teacher said, "You should talk to her, not me. I'm not the one who was offended by your behavior." The teacher went on to say, "It's important to be kind and respectful, Caleb. You never know what people are going through in their personal lives. You should not be the reason why they give up on hope."

Caleb went outside and found the new girl sitting by herself and crying. He approached her and said, "I'm sorry for being mean to you. Can we be friends?" The new girl was surprised but happy to hear that Caleb wanted to be her friend.

Caleb realized that respect for others is not just about being polite, but about valuing the worth of every person. He learned that everyone is special in their way and that it's important to treat everyone with kindness and love.

THE END

The Phenomenal Leader In Me

Example in Real Life

Jacinda Ardern is the leader of New Zealand. She thinks it's really important to be respectful to other people. That means being nice to everyone, even if they are different from you. She wants everyone to be included and treated fairly.

Ardern showed how important respect is when there was a big problem in New Zealand. In 2019, a bad thing happened, and many people were hurt. Ardern was kind to the people who were hurt and their families. She wore a special thing on her head to show she respected the people who were hurt. She made sure everyone in the country knew they were important, and that people cared about them.

Ardern always wants people to be kind to each other, no matter what they look like or where they come from. She wants everyone to feel like they belong and that they are important.

Lucie S. Matsouaka

SELF-CARE

The Phenomenal Leader In Me

Once upon a time, there was a little girl named Bintou who loved to play and have fun. Every day, she would go outside to play with her friends, go to the park, and try out new activities. But one day, Bintou noticed that she was feeling tired and run down all the time. She couldn't keep up with her friends, and even her favorite activities didn't seem as fun anymore.

Bintou went to her mom and told her what was going on. Her mom explained to her that sometimes when we are always on the go and having fun, we forget to take care of ourselves. We need to rest, eat well, and do things that make us happy and relaxed. This is called self-care.

Bintou thought about this and realized that she had been neglecting her own needs. She decided to start taking better care of herself. She would go to bed earlier, eat the healthy foods that her mom prepared for her, and take breaks to do things she loved, like reading and painting.

In no time, Bintou felt better and more energetic. She was able to play with her friends, have fun, and try new things again. She learned that taking care of yourself is one of the most important things you can do to feel happy and healthy.

THE END

Example in Real Life

Michelle Obama, who used to be the First Lady of the United States, thinks it's really important to take care of yourself. This means taking care of your body and mind, so you can be happy and feel good.

Michelle Obama talks about how she had a hard time taking care of herself when she had lots of things to do, like being a mom, a wife, and a famous person. But she learned that taking care of herself was really important and made her feel better.

Michelle Obama wants everyone to know that taking care of yourself is a good thing to do. It helps you be stronger, feel less worried and stressed, and be healthier overall. She also likes to do things like exercise, eat healthy foods, and spend time with people she cares about, as a way to take care of herself.

The Phenomenal Leader In Me

SELF-CONFIDENCE

Once upon a time, there lived a little rabbit named Mimi. Mimi was a timid and shy rabbit who was afraid of trying new things. She was always worried about what others would think of her and was scared of making mistakes.

One day, Mimi was invited to a big party hosted by the King of the forest. Mimi was excited but also very nervous about attending the party. She worried about what to wear, how to talk to the other animals, and what they would think of her.

As Mimi made her way to the party, she saw a little bird sitting on a branch looking sad. Mimi asked the bird what was wrong, and the bird replied, "I am too small to fly with the other birds. I am scared that I will never be able to fly like them."

Mimi understood how the bird felt, and she decided to help the little bird. She told the bird that he had to believe in himself and have confidence in his abilities. Mimi explained that if he believed he could fly, he would be able to fly higher than any bird in the sky.

The little bird listened to Mimi's wise words and decided to give it a try. With Mimi's encouragement, the little bird flapped his wings and soared high into the sky, and he felt proud of himself.

Seeing the little bird's success, Mimi realized that she too needed to have confidence in herself. She decided to take a deep breath, put a smile on her face, and enter the party with confidence.

As Mimi walked into the party, she saw all the animals staring at her, but instead of feeling self-conscious, she walked with confidence and greeted everyone with a smile. The other animals were happy to see her.

The Phenomenal Leader In Me

Mimi had a wonderful time at the party, and she made many new friends. She learned that having self-confidence was essential, and it allowed her to try new things, make new friends, and overcome her fears.

From that day on, Mimi was no longer a timid and shy rabbit. She was confident, brave, and always willing to try new things. She learned that having self-confidence was the key to success and that everyone can achieve great things if they believe in themselves.

THE END

Example in Real Life

Brendon Burchard is a very successful author and speaker who helps people be really good leaders. One of the things he talks about a lot is how important it is to have confidence in yourself when you're a leader. When you're confident, you're more likely to make good decisions, inspire others to do their best and bounce back when things don't go well.

Burchard thinks everyone can become more confident over time. Some things he suggests are setting goals that are achievable, celebrating when you do something well, and being kind to yourself when things don't go as planned. He also thinks it's important to have a positive attitude and see mistakes as opportunities to learn and grow.

The Phenomenal Leader In Me

SELF-DISCIPLINE

Once upon a time, there lived a little boy named Antonio. Antonio was a happy-go-lucky boy who loved playing and having fun. He had lots of friends and was loved by all the other kids in the village. But Antonio had one problem; he was very lazy and undisciplined.

Antonio used to get up late in the morning and miss his breakfast. He never completed his homework on time and was always getting scolded by his teacher. He wasted his time playing games and watching TV instead of studying.

One day at school, the principal announced that there was going to be a music concert. The music band was Antonio's favorite music band. Only the students who had turned in all their homework and who didn't miss school were going to receive a ticket.

Antonio was furious. He went home crying. "Mom, this is not fair. I want to go to the concert!" Antonio's father sat him down and said, "We've been talking to you about self-discipline and how important it is, but you're not listening. It's not completely lost, but it will require more discipline and hard work from you. If you want to achieve your goals, you'll have to get serious."

Antonio was sobbing while listening to his father. He realized that if he wanted to be successful in life, he needed to be disciplined. If he wanted to become a recipient of a free ticket to see his favorite music band, he had to stop being distracted. From that day on, Antonio started waking up early in the morning to prepare for school. He started completing his homework on time and studying regularly.

Antonio's hard work and discipline paid off. He started getting good grades in school, and his teacher was very proud of him. His friends were amazed at how much he had changed. A few months later, when the school principal announced the names of the winners, Antonio heard his name and was incredibly happy and proud of himself.

THE END

Example in Real Life

Carlos Slim is a successful businessman and philanthropist from Mexico who values self-discipline in his personal and professional life. This means he works hard, sets goals for himself, and avoids borrowing money whenever possible. He also makes sure to stay fit by exercising regularly.

Slim believes that having self-discipline is important for achieving success, both in business and in life. He encourages others to follow his lead by working hard and being responsible for their actions. Slim has also supported many educational and cultural initiatives that promote these values.

The Phenomenal Leader In Me

SELF-ESTEEM

Once upon a time, there was a little mouse named Malik. Malik lived in a beautiful grassland with all his friends. But, unlike all the other mice, Malik was always sad and down. No matter what his friends did, they could not seem to cheer him up.

One day, one of his friends asked, "Why are you always so sad?" Malik replied, "I don't like myself. I don't think I'm good enough, or smart enough, or even beautiful. Look at your beautiful fur! Mine is ugly."

His friend nodded and said, "Don't say that, Malik. Everyone is special and unique in their own way. We love your fur. You just need to believe in yourself and have self-esteem."

Malik was confused. "What is self-esteem?" His friend said, "My parents told me that self-esteem is when you believe in yourself and love yourself just the way you are." He continued saying, "See, your fur is different from mine because that's the way you were born. You're unique and I'm unique as well. We're both beautiful in our ways."

Malik smiled and decided to believe what his friend was saying about his fur. He started thinking positive thoughts about himself and soon, he felt a big change inside. He felt happier and more confident. He started to run and play with his friends, just like he used to.

Malik never forgot this lesson. He decided to love himself just the way he was and to never forget the importance of self-esteem.

THE END

The Phenomenal Leader In Me

Example in Real Life

Jim Rohn was a leader who helped people feel good about themselves. He believed that feeling good about yourself is really important if you want to be happy and successful in life. Here are some things he said to help people feel good about themselves:

First, Jim Rohn said that you should try to do things that help you grow and learn. This could be learning new skills or trying new things that are challenging. When you work hard to achieve your goals, it helps you feel proud of yourself and more confident.

Second, Jim Rohn said that you should try to spend time with people who are positive and supportive because it can help boost your self-esteem and make you feel happier.

Finally, Jim Rohn said that you should practice saying nice things to yourself. This means talking to yourself in a positive way and reminding yourself of all the good things about you. When you focus on your strengths and achievements, it helps you feel more confident and happier.

Lucie S. Matsouaka

SERVICE

The Phenomenal Leader In Me

Once upon a time, in a far-off kingdom, there was a prince named Alex. Alex was kind and generous, but he was not a typical prince. He was not interested in ruling over the kingdom with an iron fist or becoming the most powerful ruler. Instead, he wanted to serve his people and make their lives better.

One day, Alex went on a journey to visit the people in the kingdom and see how he could help. He visited villages and towns, talked to farmers, merchants, and craftsmen, and listened to their problems. He soon realized that the kingdom was facing a terrible drought, and the crops were failing. The people were going hungry, and many were leaving the kingdom in search of food.

Prince Alex knew he had to do something to help. He called upon all the people in the kingdom to come to the castle. He explained the situation and told them that he was going to lead a mission to find water and bring it back to the kingdom.

The people were amazed and inspired by Prince Alex's leadership. They joined him on the journey and worked together to find the water. They carried heavy buckets and worked tirelessly, but their spirits were high because they were doing something to help their kingdom.

After many days of searching, they finally found a river that flowed with fresh, clean water. They filled their buckets and began the journey back to the kingdom. Along the way, they encountered obstacles, such as steep mountains and raging rivers, but they never gave up.

When they finally arrived back in the kingdom, the people cheered and thanked Prince Alex for his leadership. He had led them to the water and helped them save their crops and their kingdom.

From that day on, Prince Alex was known as the servant leader of the kingdom. He continued to serve his people and lead by example, showing them that the greatest leader is one who serves.

THE END

The Phenomenal Leader In Me

Example in Real Life

George W. Bush was the 43rd President of the United States, and he thought it was really important for people to help others. He wanted everyone to do something good for their communities and make a difference in the world. To help people do this, Bush started a program called the USA Freedom Corps. He asked Americans to spend at least 4,000 hours helping others by volunteering or working in public service jobs.

Bush believed that service and helping others were important values for Americans to have. He talked about this a lot in his speeches and said that by loving our neighbors and helping each other, we can make the world a better and more hopeful place.

Lucie S. Matsouaka

CONCLUSION

Dear friend,

I'm sure you enjoyed reading all these amazing stories and also meeting a few leaders in real life who possess some of those great qualities.

In conclusion, a phenomenal leader is someone who possesses qualities such as empathy, courage, integrity, kindness, self-confidence, and so much more. If you think of any other quality that I did not mention in this storybook, please write it down and share it with people around you.

As you grow up, I hope that you will remember these stories and strive to embody these qualities in your own life. Whether you become a leader in your school, your community, the political arena, science, medical field, business, or even just among your friends and family members, you will have the tools you need to make a positive impact on the world. There is so much work to be done and I'm counting on you.

I know you'll lead by example, and you will always be willing to make tough decisions for the greater good. The qualities that make a great leader can be developed and honed with practice and determination.

Finally, you'll need to practice genuine love for people. When a leader genuinely cares about people, it becomes so much easier for him (or her) to listen to them, respect them, be kind to them, be compassionate, and serve them.

Remember, every great leader started small, but with hard work and dedication to their goals, they became the great inspirational figures that you aspire to become. So, don't be afraid to step up and lead. I do not doubt in my mind that, with a little bit of perseverance, you'll become the phenomenal leader you were created by God to be.

I love you, my friend.

Lucie

ABOUT THE AUTHOR

Lucie S. Matsouaka is an Author, International Speaker, Certified Professional Career Coach, Certified Human Rights Consultant, and a bilingual Youth Leadership Coach (French and English). Her purpose is to guide parents to better support their children's passion and nurture their dreams.

She also empowers and inspires young leaders globally by providing them with the necessary tools, resources, and opportunities to develop their leadership skills, build their confidence and cultural awareness, and positively impact both their communities and the world.

Lucie has been recognized for her work across the globe. In July 2020, after speaking to over 500 youth across the globe in Partnership with UNESCO Center for Peace, she was awarded an Official Citation from the Maryland General Assembly in recognition of her ongoing commitment to the promotion of peace and human rights.

Lucie is a diversity and inclusivity advocate who was recognized as an Amazon Best-seller for her work as a co-author with several black female authors. Her best-selling book 'Black Girls Hear' takes you through the detailed and riveting experiences of the authors and how those experiences have transformed their lives.

Lucie lives in North Carolina, USA with her husband and two children.

1

CPSIA information can be obtained
at www.ICGtesting.com
Printed in the USA
LVHW051252270723
753394LV00001B/293